# MAD HALLELUJAH

## AND OTHER ODDITIES

## OWEN MORGAN

Copyright 2019 Owen Morgan
ISBN: 9781687868091

*For Kelly,*
*For always putting up with my nonsense.*

*For Nancy,*
*For being the best thing I will ever create.*

'Big Hairy Thighs' first published in Stinkwaves Magazine
Volume 6 Issue 2
'Curse Word' first published in Dimension Bucket Magazine
Issue 1
'The Despicable Thing' first published in Dimension Bucket
Magazine Issue 1
'The Elgin Incident' first published in Aphotic Realm Magazine
Issue #3 CLASSIFIED
'Truffles' accepted for future adaptation by The NoSleep Podcast
'Suddenly Shocking'

# CONTENTS

# INTRODUCTION

The stories and poems you are about to read are, in all likelihood, going to confuse you. They are always weird, sometimes funny, invariably odd little tales that crawled out of my cranium and settled on these pages. I hope, at the very least, they entertain you.

They deal with various themes, from outright comedic to outrageously bizarre and all the way to hopelessly bleak, but I like to think that they all have their own strange *feel*. Many of them were written to strict word count limits, for various challenges and competitions, and they reflect my fascination and love for short-form storytelling.

At the end of this book I will leave you with a few notes on some of them, so stay tuned if you're interested in all that malarkey.

In the meantime, enjoy the ride.

Love and Kisses,

Owen

# THESE MAD HALLELUJAHS

Behold, these mad hallelujahs
  we scream into the dark,
  These odd and strange devotions
  to life as we depart.


Psalms of open doorways
  of closed and sightless eyes
  Where flight is yet forbidden
  for all except the flies.


Sing, o ye faithful,
  your hymns of disconcert.
  Of rot, and all unbidden
  calling from the dirt.


Take careful voyage traveler,
  on this sea of severed legs,

for the thing within the waves
persistent, pleads and begs.


Lie comfortable in velvet,
    by wood and candlelight.
    Of shovels and the men that dig,
    in the sad embrace of night.


Behold, these mad hallelujahs
    we whisper in the dark,
    these odd and strange devotions
    will tear us all apart.

# THE GREAT TRAVELLING GRAVEYARD

As the sun disappeared behind the trees, Spencer Cross sensed a change in his surroundings. A subtle odour was on the wind around Arken Township, foetid and cloying.

Spencer set down his smoking pipe, which had served well to calm his nerves, on top of a crumbling gravestone with the name 'Roland Shine' etched upon it. He wondered what sort of condition Shine's body was in, after so many months at the mercy of the worms. Would his skin be stripped away yet? He wouldn't have to wonder much longer.

Spencer had grown familiar with the distinct smell of the dead, and he noticed it now as a hungry shark might detect a drop of blood in the miasma of the ocean. He heard the restless squawking of carrion crows in the distance, a cacophonous crowd of angry, black-feathered protesters alighting upon the body of their strange, unnatural host.

It was coming.

The intermittent tremors emanating from beneath the ground were perhaps the most subtle clue of all. They were seconds apart and gentle, like the beating of a distant hollow drum. If Spencer were not leaning against the late Roland Shine's gravestone, which amplified each tremor, he would likely not have felt anything at all. The vibrations kept growing stronger and stronger as the minutes went by, a pattern that reminded Spencer of the contractions of a mother during childbirth. Excitement rose in his stomach.

It was odd that he was alone in his curiosity. Not more than two days ago he had crossed paths with a convoy of Arken's former residents as they fled, who implored him to avoid their doomed township.

"The corpseweft is coming!" They wailed, "The corpseweft will pull the dead from the earth, and when there are no more left to gather it will come for the living!"

*Corpseweft.*

It was a curious name.

Every township had its own moniker for the terror that swept through the land, but Spencer thought Arken's was by far the most poetic. It was lyrical *and* fitting, as all names should be. Yet, it was also frightening and strange. Appropriate for something that should not, by all known rules, exist. Still, despite his affection for Arken's name, he much preferred the one he himself had given it: *The Great Travelling Graveyard*. There was a sort of showmanship there, and if Spencer Cross was anything, he was a showman.

Spencer's fascination with dead things began when he was very little. He remembered with great fondness the days spent with his father, when they rose at the first sign of dawn and ventured out into dewy fields to tend to the livestock.

On particularly exciting days, they would discover one

of the ewes or lambs on the ground, ripped apart by wolves, or some other night-borne predator. He still remembered the flutter of anticipation in his stomach as they rounded up the flock, wishing — *hoping* — the head count would fall short. It was Spencer's job to bury the dead, and he took his work very seriously.

When he turned eight — old enough to carry out his duties unsupervised — Spencer would gently handle the innards, feeling their slippery, fragile wetness between his fingers. He would delve his hands deep into the carcasses, and pull out their hidden treasures. As the creature lay before him on the grass , it occurred to Spencer that the inner workings of a life were little more than a complicated and sticky jigsaw puzzle.

As a teenager, Spencer became obsessed with his morbid proclivities. He wanted to know the nature of death more than anything else, and took every opportunity to study it in all its forms. Against the urgings of his father, Spencer moved to London in order to take a low-paying job as a mortician. It was there, in London, that he would discover his true calling.

The Old Bill described Spencer's nightly outings as 'brutalism' — the savage killings of an impulsive, messy person, with no method or consistency. At first Spencer was rather insulted by this - he had always taken the greatest care in his experiments — but eventually he realised the lies were to excuse their lacklustre interest in the murders. Spencer had never been apprehended for his crimes, and he held his own theories as to why.

London - especially Whitechapel — was a brutal place, and its bowels were rich with discarded and forgotten souls. Drunkards, whores and vagrants were easy prey, and the police were not exactly bending over backwards to investigate the madman cleaning the filth from the streets.

Spencer missed London.

He couldn't help but feel a twinge of sadness that, if the rumours turned out to be true about The Great Travelling Graveyard, he would never need to take another life again.

Spencer kept his eyes fixed on the horizon.

Shortly before The Great Travelling Graveyard crested the hill, the tops of the tallest trees jostled and swayed before they fell from sight, toppling with a deafening crash. Birds abandoned their falling nests and escaped into the air like tiny puffs of black smoke, and he heard the frightened squealing of pigs on nearby farms.

Finally, the first glimpse of the beast came into view.

It was glorious.

A writhing behemoth, as tall as a castle tower and twice the width, rolled across the field like a massive black slug. Two enormous outcroppings — as dark and as undulating as the main body — took turns swinging forward, pulling the behemoth along. The heavy, heaving body carved a deep trough in the ground as it approached.

What appeared to be tiny branches protruded from all over the mass, and after a moment Spencer realised that they were not branches at all. They were limbs. Human legs and feet, arms and hands, and fingers grasping mindlessly at the air. He could make out the distant shapes of a thousand emaciated faces, mouths wide in agony, but he heard their unnatural moans filling the air.

The creature was made entirely of the reanimated dead, expunged from their resting places, clinging to each other to form a much greater horror. Arms and legs were intertwined with that of their neighbour like links in a vast and horrifying chain.

Finally, Spencer had found it.

He was excited to observe his quarry in person. Until now his experiments had proven that death was always a distinctly *final* sort of thing, but here in front of him was definitive proof to the contrary. Four months of arduous travelling, following rumours and hearsay about the *Rolling Death* or the *Ghoulball* - a name which still made Spencer chuckle - had eventually led him to it.

It grew ever closer now, a slow approach that gave him ample time to admire its form. He saw the way the bodies knitted themselves together in a homogenous, dreadful mass of death, and he remembered the name Arkenfolk had given to it.

*Corpseweft.*

It was a terrific name for such a terrible thing. Spencer was jealous he had not thought of it himself. To him, the Great Travelling Graveyard was not a monster, or a curse, or even a plague. It was a tapestry.

The ground stirred beneath his feet, and he looked down to see a pallid grey hand breach the dirt. It began clawing around for purchase in the grass.

Spencer laughed loudly and knelt beside the disembodied hand. "Mr Shine, I presume?" he said, wrapping his own hand around the dead one. A handshake, representing the union between life and death.

He tugged the cold, dead limb, freeing the whole arm up to the shoulder. A second hand emerged opposite, and then a head erupted out of the mud. For the second time today, Spencer thought about childbirth.

Roland Shine's decaying head was greyer than his rotten

hands, and the skin had putrefied. Shrivelled, milky white eyes stared at Spencer through sunken sockets, and his jaw hung low in a look of comical shock.

Spencer slid out of the way and watched Shine's body emerge fully from the grave. His legs dragged heavily on the ground behind him like two burdensome sacks of gristle and bone. More movement was occurring all around him, grave dirt displacing as the occupants escaped their resting place.

The dead were rising in their droves as if beckoned, and they all moved towards the approaching abomination. Some bodies were almost fresh — he recognised the vinegar-like smell of the preservatives — whereas others were scarcely more than skin and dust, one strong breeze away from ruin.

Spencer always knew, deep down, that death was not the true end for the human soul, but it was only at this moment that he felt validated. His whole life had led here. He would finally learn the secret of reversing death, and fulfil a promise made with his cheek pressed against his father's coffin.

Spencer followed behind the crowd of dead men and women, until they all stood directly in the path of The Great Travelling Graveyard. The ground shook tremulously with each crash of its, putrid arms, and the wailing of its cadaverous passengers became deafening. He looked up at its writhing form and saw hundreds of faces staring back at him.

Spencer smiled, and then drew the blade of his knife down both of his forearms. The lacerations were deep, and it did not take long for the blackness to fall over his eyes. As Spencer Cross bled his last into the soil, the Great Travelling Graveyard rolled over his body and woke it once more.

# CURSE WORD

Something was different about Carly today. She felt stronger.

Lee would almost certainly try to pull the wool over her eyes again, but she wouldn't let him get away with it this time. Today, she wouldn't be a sheep. She would be a *wolf*.

At first he denied it. He called Carly a jealous bitch who always blamed others for her own problems. She held her ground, showed him the photographs she had taken of his text history. His face hardened and he crossed his arms, as if this whole drama was her fault for invading his private messages.

"It's just flirting," he said. "I never met up with her."

Carly scrolled through her phone again and loaded the photos she had found in his private messages. It hurt her to look at them. She zoomed in on one, pointing out the little scar at the base of his cock he got from a biking accident when he was nineteen. He had no escape this time, literally and metaphorically caught with his pants down. There was no way to deny it, but of course he tried anyway.

Lee said that, ever since the kids, Carly had been less

interested in sex, which she admitted was true. He said Carly cared more for the twins than she did for him, which was also true. He said that Carly had let herself go, had gotten fat. This was categorically *not* true. She was a proud, fit woman even after bearing twin daughters, but Lee knew that. He only said it to hurt her feelings.

*He's just trying to push your buttons*, she tried to tell herself. But it was too late. Her button — the big flashing red one with DANGER written across it in — had been well and truly pushed.

Carly let him have it. The floodgates opened, and she spat out years of abuse and frustration like venom. She always had a foul mouth — ever since Uncle Terry stubbed his toe and shouted 'Fuck' at her sixth birthday party — but this outburst was on another level. She called Lee things that would make an Australian bricklayer blush. Veins bulged in her temples, and beads of sweat formed in the deep circles around her eyes.

Then, like a bullet fired from a rifle, she said it.

The word was foreign, and strange. It was a word she didn't recall ever hearing before that moment, but even as it left her lips she knew it was a sound that should never be spoken out loud. Something felt forbidden and dangerous about it. It rose through her feet and past her stomach, as if cast not from her mind, but from the bowels of the earth. It cleaved through the air between them, sharp and obscene.

Carly slapped a hand over her mouth, but it was futile. The word had been spoken. Lee was the intended target, and he took the full brunt of it directly between the eyes. They went wild with fright, and a split second later his face snapped backwards along the jawline, his half-decapitated head lolling from side-to-side against the back of his neck. His tongue, now exposed to the world, flapped about like a wet pink mouse trying to free itself from a trap. Lee stayed upright for a few seconds, held there by spasming muscles, before his body crumpled to the ground.

Carly screamed.

Then she vomited.

And then she screamed again. There was a sudden, cloying thickness to the air, as if a big wet slug had filled the room with its mucus. She still felt the faint electrical charge of the word, resonating on her tongue.

After a while she thought about calling the police, but she was afraid to speak out loud. Had she really killed him with a word? She tried to remember the word, but it was gone. What had it sounded like? She had no idea. It was as if the word had retreated back to wherever it came from, somewhere instinctual — primal, even — waiting to be called upon.

Carly wondered if her anger had unlocked it. Or had it been something worse, like desire? She *wanted* Lee to be punished, and now he was dead.

Carly was still shaking, but she knew what had to be done.

There had been a time once, long ago, when she had loved Lee, but Cupid's arrow had long since rusted. Now her husband was just another household chore to add to her list.

She cleaned up the mess and stored his devastated body in a chest freezer in the garage. For several weeks, she carried a small piece with her whenever she left the house. She tossed chunks of him in the river for the fish, and others she buried deep in the woods when she took the girls hiking. She made quick friends with the neighbourhood dogs - they couldn't get enough of the sweet treats she fed them through the fence cracks.

When she told her family and friends that Lee had eloped with his personal trainer, they hardly seemed surprised. Even Lee's own mother confided in Carly that her son had been 'a rotten cunt his whole life'.

Before summer was over, Lee was gone for good.

Years went by and Carly put the past behind her. Her twin girls were now in school, and she had met someone new. A man who never lied about anything or raised a hand to her. He doted on Carly and worshipped her children as if they were his own.

She hadn't cursed out loud since the day Lee died, and her temper was calmer than it ever had been.

One morning, while driving her daughters to school, a van jumped the light at an intersection and almost t-boned her. If the driver had not looked up from his phone in time, both she and her children would have been killed.

Carly, who once again felt the rage boiling inside her like hot bile, met the driver's eye through his windshield. She stepped out of her vehicle, shaking with adrenaline and shock, and so did he. The man was livid, bellowing at Carly. He said that she should be more careful, that she can't drive, that women like her should be banned from the road.

She gritted her teeth, clenched her fists...

...and let him have it.

# TRUFFLES

"Do you want some?" the boy asked. "There's plenty to share!"

I watched his little pale hands scrabble at the dirt and wondered why he was out here, so deep in the woods. He was covered head to toe in muck, and had torn a hole almost a foot down into the wet earth.

"They hide them here when it's dark," he said, his eyes wild. "But I still find them..."

"Find what?" I asked.

The little boy giggled. "The truffles, silly!"

I felt a flutter of excitement in my stomach. Truffles are worth more than gold these days. Smelly black wads of rare fungus that could pay off my mortgage, send my kids to college and buy me a fancy new sports car. Finding a truffle site in this part of the country was like falling wallet-first into your own damn goldmine.

I unclipped my hiking rucksack and dropped it onto the ground, then got on my knees beside him.

"How many have you found?" I asked, digging my fingers into the soft mud and raking a fistful of it aside.

"Plenty," the boy said, "enough for both of us to eat!"

"Oh, I won't be eating them," I said.

The boy smiled. "We'll see."

We dug for hours.

Inch-by-inch, we excavated the dirt until the small clearing looked like it had been targeted by intense mortar fire.

"Are you absolutely *sure* this is where you found some before?" I asked the boy, for what felt like the hundredth time.

"Definitely!" He said, his little arms scratching at the ground like a dog burying a bone.

He had kept up his frantic pace all day, but I was much older than him, and I felt my arms growing heavier with every passing minute. I had eaten my protein bars and drank my water hours before. My body was crying out for sustenance. I wanted to stop, but I told myself I would not give up until I had a pocket full of those smelly black diamonds.

They were calling out for me, from deep inside the earth.

By the time night fell, my hands were numb and bloody and caked in muck.

The boy was still crouched down, furiously searching, except he was naked now. Had he been naked when we first met on the trail? It had been so long ago.

I scraped another handful of dirt from the hole, and my

fingernail snapped backwards against a rock buried within the mud. I winced, expecting pain, but there was none. My hands were too cold to feel anything.

I plucked off the dangling cuticle and popped it in my mouth. *Waste not, want not.* It tasted of nothing except grit and blood, but it woke a hunger in my belly that whispered and begged and would not be denied.

The morning sunrise brought with it a torrential downpour.

My clothes were drenched, so I removed them all and tossed them away. The slick mud felt wonderful on my bare skin, somehow primal and ancient, as if I had slaked an inexorable urge I never knew I had.

I was still hungry. So hungry that my stomach twisted and wrenched in distress. The boy seemed content with the worms, peeling them from the earth and slurping them down like writhing strings of pink spaghetti, but I craved something more.

I looked at my hands.

The broken skin on my fingers had first turned blue and then eventually black. They stank of something sweet and musty and tempting, like off-meat.

I felt nothing when I bit down on my thumb, yet the skin split and the bone cracked in my teeth with relative ease. I swallowed the sour, cold chunk. When it slipped down my throat, I could almost hear my stomach whispering gratefully.

"Hey, can you smell that?" The boy asked.

I heard him snuffling against the ground like an excited sow. "Quick! I think I've found one!"

I rose to my feet and looked across the clearing. The boy was hopping in the air and waving his hands, his skinny body almost translucent in the moonlight. I felt a rush of delight fill me up like thick, hot cement.

How long had we been burrowing in the mud? Days? Weeks? It felt as if I had never been anywhere but here, down amongst the insects, searching. Would my wife be looking for me? I supposed it didn't matter, she would understand my absence when I returned bearing our fortune in fungus.

"Come on, silly, help me get it out!" The boy called.

I climbed out of my hole and ran as fast as I could on trembling, exhausted legs. The boy was heaving something from the ground. Massive and dark and long. If it really *was* a truffle, it would be worth more than I could imagine.

I reached out to offer my hands, but in my excitement I had forgotten that they were mostly gone. Over the last day and night I had chewed the sweet-smelling black meat from every one of my fingers, leaving only the jagged bones jutting from my tattered skin. I would never again be able to grip anything in my decimated hands, but the exposed, skeletal prongs were ideal for raking the dirt.

"Isn't it a beauty?" The boy asked, pulling the enormous object free of its resting place. "Hidden here in the woods, forgotten. Wasted!"

I looked on in wonder, my stomach growling. "Who would discard such a thing?"

The boy knelt down and took a gigantic bite out of our earthy jackpot, groaning in satisfaction. I started to salivate.

"Try some," The boy said, pulling me down beside him. "It's to die for!"

The same slightly foul, fascinating odour that had emanated from my dead fingers was now filling the air with temptation. The sweet smell of decay.

There was no way I could sell something so exquisitely appetising.

When my teeth sunk into the fragile flesh and my mouth filled with its aromatic juices, I groaned too. The flavour. It was divine!

We feasted until our truffle was stripped down to its alabaster bones. We cracked them between our teeth and teased out the marrow with our probing tongues. We ate and ate, morsel by mouth-watering morsel, yet still we were hungry.

I plucked out the milky, sunken eyes and swallowed them like raw oysters. We drank the thick, clotted blood like wine. We broke open the swollen belly and savoured the succulent treasures within, even though most of it had already been claimed by the worms.


It took us the best part of a day to devour the whole thing. Our bellies were distended and full of the rich, forbidden delicacies. The boy and I wasted no time, and started to dig again.

I had never eaten truffles before, but now I couldn't imagine eating anything else.

## THE BALLAD OF SLIPPERY RHYS

THIS IS THE BALLAD OF SLIPPERY RHYS,
    who was born all covered in grease.
    It softened his flesh and his bones turned to dough,
    so he could squeeze into crevice or crease.


He had a peculiar trick where he made himself slick
    and slid under windows and doors.
    He would flatten right down to the girth of a pound
    and flap his flat limbs on the floor.


Despite this incredible gift,
    it was a matter of 'when' and not 'if'
    Reese would turn his attention to crime,
    but The Flat Bandit was captured with nary a fuss,
    cause the police tracked the trail of slime.

. . .

A jury decreed he should hang for his deeds,
    for they could not have a freak such as he loose.
    Eventually though, they just let him go,
    'cause his neck wouldn't stay in the noose.

# THE CLUMP

HOWARD KISSED HIS WIFE ON THE CHEEK AS SHE LEFT FOR work, blissfully unaware that his morning was going to suck more than any morning has ever sucked, anywhere, ever.

"Gotta go, I'm already late," Allie said, her breath clouding in the frosty air. "Don't forget to put out the recycling!"

She hooked a thumb at the table next to the door, empty cans and old cardboard packages stacked in a treacherously tall pile.

"Got it." Howard said, yawning.

"And for fuck's sake brush your teeth!"

Howard yawned again, this time blowing a hot morning breath in her direction. Allie squealed in disgust and skipped into street, her shoes crunching on the frozen morning dew.

"You're vile!" She announced.

"Bye babe." Howard said.

She adjusted the bobble hat on her head, making sure her ears were tucked underneath the thick cotton. "Try not to break anything."

"I'll try."

Allie waved goodbye as she hurried off towards her car, and Howard shut the door.

He put his hands in the air and stretched, twisting his back from side to side until there was a loud crack. Then he did the same with his neck until a joint cracked in there too. He sighed in relief. *I'm falling to god-damn pieces*, Howard thought.

Every morning his bones screamed him awake, and his skeleton felt about as structurally sound as the pile of recycling next to the door, which he would inevitably forget to take outside. He rubbed at his neck and decided a hot shower would help soothe his aches, not to mention wash away the sweat and farts from his (and, despite her vigorous denials, Allie's) night-time emissions.

Howard's knees popped in rhythm with every step of the staircase. He shed his dressing gown, t-shirt, and boxer shorts as he ascended, until he stood on the landing proudly naked aside from a pair of mismatched Marvel socks. Captain America and Thor stared up at his crotch with smouldering intensity, neither hero balking at the sight of the tremendous nemesis before them.

He lifted his feet one by one and ripped the socks off, discarding them over his shoulder. They flopped softly into little heaps on the ground. Lord Penis had won, the Avengers defeated once and for all.

Howard stepped into the shower and cranked the water on. The old boiler downstairs — which had been installed sometime during the Cretaceous period — groaned loudly as it sputtered to un-life, and the shower head rattled against the tiles when the first drops were dispensed. Howard leaned his nude body away from the water, giving it time to go from glacially cold to blisteringly hot — the only two temperatures the boiler could manage — before he stepped into the flow.

Every time Howard took a shower, he remembered exactly how much he hated showering. He had always been more partial to a nice hot bath. In his opinion, there was something to be said about being warmly embraced by water, rather than mercilessly pelted by it.

He watched the suds roll down his legs, and saw that the water was pooling under his feet instead of going down the drain. Through the soap, he could make out something dark stuffed around the metal sprues of the drain, blocking it. He bent lower and peered at the foreign mass, swiping away the soapy water to get a better look.

It looked like some kind of black hair coiled around the plug hole, but that couldn't be right. He called his wife 'blondie' occasionally for a very good reason (she was blonde) and he was tormented throughout his childhood due to the zestiness of his own orange bonce.

So whose hair could it be?

A sudden nightmare scenario hacked into his head like an axe through a screen door, and his eyes widened.

*Oh god, please don't let it be a fucking massive spider*, he thought.

Howard stopped the water and squatted over the plug, looking around for something he could use to wedge the blockage out. Allie's disposable razor was resting on the back of the sink, so he leaned over and picked it up. He hooked a few strands of the fibres with the hard plastic handle and pulled. The clump started to move, coming up easily at first, in thick, gooey black strands. Howard gagged at the smell -- a mix of sewage, meat and something mustier, like wet earth.

The clump of hair tugged back.

His hand jerked violently, and the flimsy plastic razor began to bend. Howard panicked and tried to seize the thing as it snapped back down into the drain. He managed to catch a loop of fibrous hair with his index finger, surprised at his own lightning reflexes, only... something wasn't right.

The clump was once again wrapped tightly in the drain, but now there was a new object resting on top of it, oval shaped and wet. It looked almost like a boiled sweet, or an olive, but that was impossible.

No.

Last time Howard checked, olives didn't have fingernails on them.

Howard looked at his hand and saw that his index finger was now three-quarters-of-an-inch shorter than it had been moments before, and blood was leaking from his severed fingertip in dark red rivulets.

"Huh." Howard said with almost casual surprise, then fainted.

He woke up face down on the bathroom floor, his head fuzzy and his hand throbbing. He felt nauseous, and when he looked down he saw a large red bloodstain on the bath mat.

*Shit*!

The area where his finger tip should have been was unoccupied, and below it was a clean slice, as if someone had swung a finely crafted katana at it. His hand was caked with dark red blood, but the flow had slowed to an almost casual sputter from the tip every few seconds. He felt the blackness creeping over him again and he slapped himself in the face, hard. The blackness retreated, and he tried to think.

What did the doctors on *Casualty* do in situations like this? *God fucking damn it, think*. He pressed his foot into the bath mat and the blood squelched up to meet his toes. He had lost a lot, enough to saturate the mat, so the priority now was to keep as much blood as possible *inside* his body.

He had to find something to tie off the flow to his finger. He tried to think of the word they used on TV, but his head was still woozy and all he could come up with were the words 'turnip' and 'croquet'.

He stumbled onto the landing, looking for something long and pliable he could use as a croquet. He remembered that his phone was plugged into the wall, and yanked the charger cable free from its adapter. The phone careened across the landing, disappearing somewhere amongst a large pile of laundry at the top of the staircase.

He tied the cable around the base of his finger and tightened it with his teeth. The end of his finger screamed its disapproval and gave a protesting spit of blood, until finally the pressure gave way to numbness.

He breathed in relief, picked up a wayward sock off the floor -- *Captain America, at your service* -- and gripped it tightly against his wound. He was shaking uncontrollably now, the adrenaline petering off.

Howard put the lid of the toilet seat down and sat heavily on top of it.

What was happening? What the hell was that thing in his shower drain? It seemed possible that it was an animal, but he had never seen anything like it before. Besides, who deals with killer plug hole monsters these days? Pest control? The council? The *Ghostbusters*? This was certainly strange *and* it was occurring in his neighbourhood, so it was well within their jurisdiction.

Another logical option would be to burn down the whole fucking house, but honestly it was hard enough getting on the property ladder as it is, without setting fire to the bottom rung.

First things first though, he was going to call an ambulance and get his finger looked at. Or, he would have done that, were he able to find his phone.

It had flung off somewhere when he pulled it from the charger, and he hadn't seen where it had landed. He always told Allie that they didn't need a landline because the only people that still call those things were their grandparents (all of whom were long dead) and cold-call telemarketers (all of whom should be dead). He hadn't ever considered the possibility of losing both his fingertip and his mobile phone within the space of two minutes.

Howard looked at the bloodied sock in his hand and pondered the various ways his life would be changed without the very tip of his index finger, when he suddenly realised they could probably stick it back on. They could do that, right? He was sure he had read about people losing toes and even whole limbs, and the boffins at the hospital just plonked it right back on for them, good as new. He just needed to get the tip on ice to preserve it.

He stood up and peered into the bath. His errant digit was still there, which was a good start, but it was right on top of the plug hole, resting on the dark clump of hair.

"Okay, little guy" he said to the detached chunk of flesh. "I'm coming for ya."

He gathered his courage and proceeded to try and flick the fingertip out of the plug hole and into the opposite end of the bath, where he could safely reach in and grab it. But as soon as his hand got close, one of the strands of black hair shot up from the drain and whipped at him.

"Ow!" He yelled, reeling back. A burning sensation shot across his palm, where there was now a thin slice right through the flesh. The skin split into an angry red rift when he stretched his hand, but it didn't bleed. It was like a massive paper cut, and he grit his teeth through the disproportionately painful sting.

"Okay, that's it. I'm done with this," he announced.

Howard stormed downstairs, passed through his kitchen and opened the door to the garden. He was about to step out into the cold when he remembered he wasn't wearing any shoes. Or trousers. Or indeed, anything else besides the Captain America sock clenched around his wounded finger.

Howard turned and stormed back upstairs again. He grabbed the nearest item of clothing, which happened to be Allie's sherbet pink dressing gown, threw it around his back and slipped his arms through the sleeves. They barely came down past his forearm, and the rest of the gown struggled to stretch around his generous midriff. When he tied up the waistband it appeared more like a preposterous smoking jacket, but it covered his genitals and would do the job for now.

He ran back downstairs, crossing the lawn to a small tool-shed. He pulled open the door and searched amongst the debris for his flat head screwdriver. Finally, after he had been out in the cold long enough for his testicles to retreat entirely inside his body, he saw the screwdriver poking out from a half crushed cardboard box. He snatched it out, adjusted the pink gown — which had ridden up so high that the belt was now around his midriff — and hurried back inside the house. He also made a mental note to sort out the shed, which he knew full well he would never bother to do.

When he reached the bathroom again he dropped to his knees and jammed the tip of the flathead under the lip of the metallic drain cover. His palm stung like hell from the cut, and it was now seeping blood from the thin slit. The drain cover was tight against the ceramic of the bath, but a slight — and very painful — whack with his other hand helped wedge it under the rim. While he did this, the black hairy thing whipped its strands at his hand, giving him a series of tiny cuts across his knuckles. He grimaced at the pain and looked at his former fingertip, still abandoned on the drain, staring at him accusingly with its filthy and badly trimmed nail, and the anger rose again.

*Fuck this thing.*

Howard yanked up on the handle of the screwdriver, and after a series of cracks the whole drain popped free. He lifted it slowly, bringing the entire clump with it. The thing was huge, an enormous wodge of pitch black gunge that just kept coming. It must have been eight inches long, it's disgusting mane of hair dripping wet and half coated in soapy bubbles. The smell was horrendous, like low tide at anus beach, but that wasn't the worst thing about the clump. The worst was the legs, countless pairs of them running along each side, flailing in segmented waves like an enormous centipede.

He was so mesmerised by the hypnotic movement of the legs that he failed to even notice the bulbous head of the thing whipping from side to side and probing the air with two long barbed antennae. The mouth was horrifically large, a sickening maw with four serrated mandibles. It opened to let out a piercing shriek.

Howard responded to the sudden sound by squealing at almost exactly the same pitch, and instinctively dropped the whole mess back into the bath. He fell backwards, smacking his spine against the rim of the toilet and knocking the wind out of himself. The clump was still screeching and flailing, throwing water everywhere.

The screwdriver shot up in the air, and then the recently detached plug hole followed. Finally, something small and oval and red, which he recognised as his former fingertip, sailed overhead, landing with a soft plop into the toilet bowl.

Howard looked up at the ceiling and sighed. Turning his back on the bath, where the creature still thrashed and screeched, he looked into the toilet bowl.

His erstwhile extremity rested just inside the curve of the u-bend, so he plunged his left hand into the water. The slashes on his hand were gently weeping blood, and it clouded out in thin tendrils of red as he reached towards his prize. One of his fingers knocked its fallen comrade clumsily, nudging it deeper into the bend, but after some very careful and uncharacteristic dexterity, Howard was able to grab it.

He pulled his hand out, laughed triumphantly and kissed the fingertip like it was a piece of priceless treasure. Then he remembered where it had just been and retched loudly.

As he held back the vomit, he sensed that something wasn't right. It was quiet now, almost silent. There was no scratching, scraping or screeching. He leapt to his feet and looked in the bath, horrified.

It was empty.

Howard's heart skipped so many beats that when it eventually started again his toes began to tingle. He frantically scanned the room for signs of where the clump had gone.

There was a thin trail of water from the rim of the bath, leading out of the door and across the landing. He cautiously followed it, shaking with every step, until the trail stopped in front of the laundry pile.

*Hide and seek*, thought Howard. He kicked the pile of clothes hard, and a muffled screech came from inside. Howard took that as his cue, and jumped feet first onto the pile. The screeching got louder, so he jumped again. Then again. And again. He jumped up and down on the mound of clothes like he was a kid testing out his new wellingtons in a muddy puddle. The noises ceased after a few more stomps, and eventually so did Howard's athletics.

He puffed and wheezed for a short few moments (such was the limitations of his cardio) and then began to pluck items of clothing from the pile. He hoped the creature hadn't burst open the way cockroaches do when you step on them. A lot of the laundry was Allie's nice clothes, and she would never believe him if he told her a giant bug had expunged its innards all over them. He moved a blouse and caught a glimpse of black hair resting motionless on a pair of jeggings.

"Ha HA!" He exclaimed in victory. "How'd you like that?"

In response, the mound of hair shifted and jumped with incredible speed, uncoiling like a spring. Howard had just enough time to see the nightmare image of a hundred flailing legs and snapping mandibles as they hurtled toward him, before it clamped over his face like a mandatory Halloween mask.

He tried to scream but his mouth wouldn't open. The smooth, segmented underbelly rubbed against his nose and chin - cold and wet sheets of chitinous bone that made him gag at their touch. The thing's barbed legs had sunk into the flesh of his cheeks. He poked vainly at them with his fingers, hoping to find purchase. The creature clenched its body tighter, squeezing his lips together so hard that he started to drool.

Howard lost his footing, and the series of tumbling thuds and painful bounces that followed told him with a high degree of certainty that he had just fallen backwards down the stairs. After what seemed like an eternity, he finally slammed onto the floor in the hallway and groaned.

The clump enjoyed the fall about as much as he had, and it detached from his face with a deflated squeal. Howard gasped for air as the creature scuttled off into the kitchen. He gathered himself up to follow it, plucking a few strands of black hair out of his mouth.

Howard watched the clump skitter across the room, it's bony legs clicking in staccato rhythm against the hard tile floor. He picked up a nearby shoe and threw it, but he missed the clump by a country mile. It's unpredictable zig-zagging meant the next shoe also failed to connect, and he instead looked around for another weapon.

When he was fifteen, Howard's father had bought him a cricket bat. The same bat now caught his eye, leaning against the radiator beside the front door.

He snatched it by the handle, and carefully wrapped his right hand around it. His missing fingertip screamed in pain and squirted a small gout of blood in protest, but Howard smiled anyway. The bat was scuffed and scratched and covered in various nicks and dents from a career hitting solid balls across dirty fields. Now, it would be starting a new career, this time in the pest extermination business.

By this point, Howard was fuelled by simple bloodlust, and he stormed into the kitchen.

The clump squealed hideously and scurried towards the kitchen units, trying the find a nook or cranny big enough to squeeze into. He swung the bat and missed, hitting nothing but ceramic floor tile with a woody clank. The vibration of the hit sent waves of pain up his arms and through his joints.

The creature shot across the floor with blinding speed, like a vile little cruise missile, leaving a filthy trail as its damp black hair dragged behind it. Howard swung again.

This time he only narrowly missed, hitting one of the cupboard doors with a sonorous crack, breaking the veneer and burying the edge of the bat into the hollow core. The clump turned to face him and rose on its haunches, hissing at him like a threatened snake.

Howard winced away from the creature, more out of disgust than fear. It made his skin crawl in a way he couldn't control, as if it triggered some sort of primal reaction. He tugged at his weapon but it was wedged in the cupboard door, and the creature took the opportunity to gallop past him on its abhorrent, numerous legs.

"Oh no you don't," Howard said.

He wrapped both hands around the bat and pulled with all the strength he could muster. The door splintered and the bat came free. The clump was scuttling through the hall again, and Howard rushed after it. He knew if it got ahead of him and found a hiding place, he'd never find it again. He swung his weapon in a huge overhead arc, hoping to bring it down right on the thing's head, but his attack was cut short when the bat connected far too early on the upper frame of the kitchen doorway.

Howard looked up just in time to read the brand name on the flat side of the wood, as it came down on his forehead with a hollow clack. The unexpected impact made his eyes blur, and his ears rang like a struck tuning fork.

He collapsed forward into the hallway, dazed and disoriented, and decided that he had found the perfect spot for a nice lie down.

His heart beat in his chest like the brass section of an unco-ordinated marching band, and his brain felt like it was being slowly pushed onto a bed of nails. He had entirely forgotten about the creature, until it skittered past him into the shoe rack under the staircase. He fumbled after it with his maimed hand, but his depth perception had undergone a catastrophic malfunction.

Howard lay there for several seconds, his breathing laboured and gasping, when he sensed a sudden burst of cold air and light.

The front door had opened.

Through the tinny whistling in his ears, he heard a voice. "Oh no sweetheart..."

It was Allie. She was home.

"Babe?" Howard said, confused.

"Oh my... what has he done to you?" Allie cooed.

Howard mumbled incoherently. "It hurt me... it's a... a... *gross*... I don't know what..."

"Oh you poor thing," She said, kneeling. Howard raised his hand expectantly, wanting her to touch him and tell him he was okay, but then he realised she wasn't looking at him. She wasn't *talking* to him.

Howard heard an excited squeak from inside one of his work boots, and watched as the creature unfurled from within. It sauntered over to Allie, who held out one of her hands.

"Don't, it's dangerous!" Howard tried to say, but his mouth melded the words into one drooling stream of unintelligible sounds.

The creature walked onto Allie's hand and climbed up to her shoulder. She removed her bobble hat. Her hair, beautiful and blonde, cascaded out in bouncing curls, all except for one patch on the side of her head.

Instead of hair, Howard saw a large rectangular section of angry red flesh, raw and glistening like a piece of uncooked steak. There were small holes along each edge of the deep wound, evenly spaced apart.

"What happened to your head?" Howard reached towards her, but the creature, now on her shoulder, turned and screeched at him. He pulled his hand away in revulsion.

Allie shushed the creature, and reached up to stroke its hairy back like an absurdly ugly dog. The creature settled at her touch and chittered happily. It was a noise that made Howard feel nauseous.

It climbed onto Allie's head and settled its body into the gap in her hair, legs sliding perfectly into the holes like a docking station. The stringy black hair on the creatures back was now intermingled with Allie's lush blonde hair, and Howard watched in horror as it slowly changed colour to blend in with the rest. The black gave way to a shimmering golden sheen that travelled down to the tips, as if someone had poured a tin of yellow paint over her head.

The creature was gone now, blended into Allie like the missing piece in a jigsaw puzzle.

Howard panted heavily, unable to catch his breath.

"I know this must be a lot to take in," Allie said finally, seeing the catatonic expression on his face. "But you were never supposed to find out about this."

"Wh... what... are you?" Howard stammered.

"I'm your wife, silly!" smiled Allie. "This doesn't have to change anything, I still love you very much, and you'd be pretty shallow to let something like this come between us!"

"You're not *human*..."

Allie tilted her head thoughtfully.

"I guess not, but I'm still a person. I'm certainly not some sort of monster!"

"But that thing in the drain..."

"Oh is that where he was? He must have fallen out while I was in the shower. I was in such a hurry I didn't even notice!" She laughed, as if this whole thing was nothing more than a hilarious lark. Howard didn't laugh, he just stared, dumbfounded. Allie took his hand in hers.

"He's a part of me. One of many. We have a, uh..." she thought for a moment. "I guess you'd call it a 'symbiotic relationship'."

Howard pulled his hand away. "One of many?"

Allie ignored him. "What happened to your finger?"

Howard frowned, piecing together the following absurd sentence in his head: "Your hair chopped it off."

She smiled. "Well, we can't tell that to the Emergency Room staff can we? Come on, we'll think of something on the way. You didn't happen to keep your finger did you?"

Howard reached into the pocket of the sherbert pink dressing gown and pulled the fingertip out. It was already starting to smell weird.

"Great!" Allie said, grinning. "I know every inch counts to you."

Howard wanted to laugh. He always laughed at Allie's jokes. But this time he couldn't.

Allie helped him to his feet and got him appropriately dressed in lounge pants and an old *Butthole Surfers* T-shirt. She put the severed fingertip in a Tupperware container full of ice and sealed it with tape. Howard had the horrible thought that this wasn't her first time doing this.

As they went out the door, Allie spotted a large and intricate cobweb extending across the aperture above her head. In the middle of it sat a particularly fat looking orb weaver, waiting patiently for a fly to entangle itself in its trap.

Allie reached up, plucked the plump little creature from its web and popped it casually into her mouth. Howard heard it crunch between her teeth, and saw a gout of creamy white guts rolling around on her tongue as she chewed.

"I guess we can finally be ourselves around each other from now on." Allie said, shivering with excitement at the prospect. A single, crooked spider leg poked from her lips like a skinny tree branch.

"It feels so... *liberating!*"

# KIDDO

"I KNOW WHAT YOU'RE THINKING, KIDDO," AMBER SAID, HER painted eyes content and calm and somehow still joyful. "You've gotta do it. I understand."

I started to cry. It was getting so cold. The snow had piled up over the door now, and still it fell.

"But," I said, choking back tears. Amber and I have been together for as long as I can remember—ever since Mommy brought her back from the market when I was three years old. "You're my best friend…"

"I know I am. You're my best friend too," she said. "We've had some good times, haven't we?"

"If you go, who else will be my friend?" I whimpered. The heat from the log burner was fading fast, so I huddled closer. Close enough to wrap my arms around it. I didn't though, Mommy told me never to touch it because I would burn myself.

Amber chuckled. She sounded so funny when she laughed. "If I *don't* go, neither of us will have any friends at all, ever again!"

I didn't laugh with her; I was too sad.

Amber must have noticed, because her voice softened again. "Let me help, and at least you might stay warm for a few more hours. Long enough for someone to come."

She was right. She was always right. It's just that I *couldn't* do it. But what choice do I have? All Mommy's books are gone, already burnt in the fire. I looked high and low for wood; I even burnt the little chair I sat on for my dinner. There are other wooden chairs too, but they are big and heavy and I'm not strong enough to break them. Mommy is still sleeping and I can't wake her up to help, no matter how hard I shake her.

But maybe I won't have to burn anything else! The snow can't last much longer, can it? Daddy would be back soon, wouldn't he? Mommy said he was stuck in the blizzard too, but maybe he got out. Maybe he was on his way here right now.

Maybe he wasn't.

"Whadya say, kiddo?" Amber asked, startling me from my thoughts. She was always so smart, and she was a good friend. My *best* friend. "I'll keep the fire burning for as long as I can. You'll be okay, I promise."

"I guess so ..." I said, wiping away the tears.

When I picked Amber up and brushed her thick orange hair with my trembling hand, I noticed one of my fingers turning blue. Amber's little painted smile was still there, curling upward into her freckly red cheeks. It had faded over the years, because I took her everywhere with me.

"I love you, Ambie." I said, giving her one last kiss.

"Love you too, kiddo," she replied.

I opened the heavy metal door and dropped her in. Her red-and-white polka dot dress caught first, then the rest of her little wooden body went up too.

# FLOWER OF FLESH AND BLOOD

SAM WATCHED THE OTHER CHILDREN MEETING THEIR PARENTS at the school gate, mums and dads kneeling to greet their sons and daughters. Some parents held their kids' hands as they walked, others tried but were met with the mortified expressions of their too-cool pre-teens. Sam slunk past them all and made his way home alone.

When he arrived, his mother was in the front garden tending to her rose bush. Sam knew precious little about his mother, but he knew not to bother her when she was gardening. The only time he had ever seen his mother smile with any sincerity was while she was holding a pair of secateurs, and during those brief moments she could almost pass as a normal human being.

Sam took a deep breath, then opened the front gate and scurried past. He almost made it to the door when his mother spun around and caught him by the arm. Blossom wasn't a large or imposing woman, but her sinewy arms were toughened by age and graft, giving her a strong grip that was not easily slipped. Sam lowered his head as she studied him curiously, a bird of prey eyeing its next meal.

"There's a corned beef sandwich on the side," She said, letting him go. "Eat it and then go to your room. I'm busy and I don't want to see you until supper."

"Yes mother."

She released his arm, and he could feel her watching as he rushed into the house. A wave of relief washed over him, not because he was back home, but because there was a wall separating them, at least for the time being.

The sandwich was a bland affair, amounting to little more than one thick slice of corned beef slapped between two thin pieces of white bread. No butter, no dressing, no salad. He spiced it up by squirting a small amount of ketchup on it, spreading it over the beef with one finger. He had to be careful when he took something without permission. Sam ate the sandwich, washed up his plate and retired to his room. Although denied a television, he could keep books, and he found enough life amongst the pages to make his own bearable.

He ran a finger across the spines on his bookshelf. Many of them were tattered and misshapen, read and re-read not only by him but countless others before him. In a funny way, Sam supposed they were sort of kindred spirits, sharing the same journey, reading the very same pages they had once read in their own houses and in their own times. His finger stopped on *The Hobbit* by JRR Tolkien.

He plucked it from the shelf, flopped onto his bed and began reading. The soft clicking of his mother's secateurs as they snipped branches and dead flower heads floated in through the open window, providing a monotonous soundtrack. Before long he was in Middle Earth with Bilbo and the dwarves, and much to the hobbit's dismay, they were off to kill a dragon.

The vague hum of voices outside pulled him from the book around an hour later, and he set it aside to see what was happening. His window was small, but it overlooked the street. His mother stood at the garden gate, speaking with another woman of a similar age. She took off her gardening gloves and shook the woman's hand, a wide, insincere smile occupying her face like graffiti on the side of a condemned building. Sam didn't know who the other woman was, but he recognised the girl holding her hand. It was Sandy from Maths class.

Sandy had changed out of her uniform and was now wearing a pretty floral summer dress. She had also discarded the ponytail, opting for a pair of pigtails that hung over each shoulder like foxtails. He liked Sandy. She was the only person that ever really made an effort to talk to him, and when she did, she actually listened to what he had to say.

Sandy looked nervous, and Sam saw she was holding a small, colourful box wrapped up with ribbons. The other woman — presumably Sandy's mother — spoke for a few moments, then Blossom shook her head gravely, and gestured towards Sam's bedroom window. All three looked up at the same time and Sam panicked, backing out of sight.

After a few more minutes talking, Sandy reluctantly handed the box to Blossom and the two visitors left. Sandy looked up at his window one last time as they walked away, disappointment etched on her face.

Sam sighed.

He fished a pen from his school bag and walked over to the Marvel Comics calendar on his wall. There was only a single significant date on it. He drew a diagonal line through today's box, in which he had drawn the number '12' in felt-tip pen.

"Happy Birthday," he said to himself, and went back to reading.

When 7pm came, Sam made his way downstairs for supper. In the kitchen there was another sandwich — this time containing two sad looking pieces of cheap cheese and nothing else. He sat at the kitchen table alone and ate it, listening to the muffled sound of voices and telltale lights flickering in the living room. His mother sat in front of the television for hours every night, but it was difficult to tell whether she enjoyed it. Blossom would stare at the screen, watching the programmes from beginning to end without ever changing the severe expression on her face. Sam had recently settled on the notion that she wasn't just watching the people on screen, she was *studying* them, and that frightened him.

Blossom was different outside the house. Whenever someone visited, she would slip into a pre-prepared character, on a stage no-one else could see. As soon as they were alone again the facade would slip away, like rotten meat off the bone. Something was wrong with his mother, and Sam didn't understand it.

He was washing the crumbs off his plate when the muffled sounds of the television abruptly quieted.

"Sam?"

Sam hesitated, wondering if he could successfully sneak away, but ultimately decided against it.

"It's me mother," he said.

"Good. Come here, will you?"

Her voice was soft, which was unusual. When he walked into the living room he saw his mother sat in her usual reclining armchair, lit dimly by the artificial glow of the television. A thin nightgown covered her bony frame, and she held a glass of wine in one hand. A slim trail of smoke rose to the ceiling, coming from the cigarette resting between her lips.

Sam stopped in the doorway.

"Come closer."

He stepped forward. She set down the wineglass and picked up a piece of paper from her lap. He took it and saw that it was a crumpled ten pound note.

"Happy Birthday," she said.

"Thank you," he smiled, knowing full well that she had forgotten all about it. Sandy's visit had reminded her. He waited for her to mention Sandy, but she just clicked the remote and un-muted the tv, watching the actors in some brightly lit soap opera engaging in their own personal dramas.

"Has anyone else called to see me?" he blurted, in a tone that clearly tipped his hand. His mother turned to him, her face crumpled in a frown. She plucked the cigarette from her lips and smirked.

"Just some whore. Wanted to know if you were having a party." She took a long drag on the cigarette and exhaled. "I told her you weren't well."

"Sandy isn't a whore," he said, outrage welling in the pit of his stomach. "She's nice. Why did you tell her that?"

"Because girls like that will tempt you. They'll play with your mind and turn it to mush. I won't allow it."

"But—"

"But nothing." She pointed her crabby hand at him, the end of the cigarette between her fingers glowing softly. "A whore like that tempted your father too, and now he's dead because of it." Blossom sounded calm, but her upper lip flicked up into a momentary snarl as she spoke. It was a very small tell, but Sam was familiar with it.

"Okay mum, I'm sorry," he said, yielding the battle before it became a war.

She gestured at the note in his hand. "Put that money somewhere safe."

"I will."

As Sam walked back to his room he wondered where his mother might have hidden Sandy's gift. He decided he would wait for his mother to go to bed and look for it then.

It was nearly midnight when he heard the unmistakable shuffling of slippers past his bedroom, and he gave it another half an hour beyond that before getting out of bed.

He had been through this mission several times before, often to steal a slice of bread or a glass of milk while the coast was clear, but he had never been out more than a few minutes. If he was ever caught...

He just wouldn't *get* caught, he decided.

The door to his room creaked when it opened too far, so he cracked it only wide enough for him to squeeze through into the hall. He tip-toed along the edge of the wall, and counted the steps as he descended the staircase.

One.

Two.

Three.

Four.

On step five there would be a very loud creak, so he braced his hand on the wall and leapt from one side of the hall to the other, landing as softly as possible. When his feet touched the cold tiles of the kitchen floor, he was safe.

He yawned hard and began searching for the gift box. He started by looking under Blossom's chair, but found nothing except an empty cigarette packet and a warren of woolly dust bunnies. The cupboards in the living room were equally barren, aside from the locked drinks cabinet, which he could see through the glass was fully stocked. Fitting an average sized gift in there alongside the alcohol would have been an impressive feat in itself. Sam went back into the kitchen to comb through the cupboards. He spotted his mother's secateurs resting near the sink, and on the worktop around them was a litter of small white shapes. Little triangles and squares of paper, all with words printed on them, some of them still clinging to the curved blades of the secateurs. The trail of shapes led to the bin beneath the counter.

He pressed his foot gently on the pedal. The lid rose and showed a pile of shredded paper; a mountain of hacked words resting on top of old food and empty wine bottles. Sam took a handful out and laid them on the table, trying to figure out what it was. Finally, he found a large piece with words he recognised: '*Treasure Island*'. Sam thought of Sandy, handing over a small package with the dimensions of a book to his mother, and grit his teeth so hard that they squeaked against each other in the back of his mouth.

Pure rage welled up inside him like the foam in a shaken soda bottle. How could she do this? She hadn't just thrown it away or hidden it, she'd hacked it to pieces; destroyed something meant for him, something he would have cherished, something given to him by the only person he could ever even *describe* as friendly. He pulled as much as he could from the bin and placed it inside a plastic bag.

She might have stopped him reading it, but she wouldn't

stop him owning it. He would put it someplace she would never find it. That way, he would know he had beaten her.

But that wasn't enough. He was still angry.

*He* wanted to take something from *her*.

Sam was woken the next morning by a scream. He sat bolt upright in bed, his brain still groggy and his eyes stinging. There was banging, crashing and shouting coming from downstairs, and what he had done the night before came flooding back.

Now he was afraid.

A door slammed and feet thudded on the staircase. They made the landing and a few stomps later stopped at his door. It swung open and his mother stood there, her face twisted in fury. Blood ran down her arms, and it took him a while to understand what she was holding. It was the branches of the rose bush he had sliced away in the night, each one with a withering flower at the tip. The thorns pierced her hands, but she held them tight regardless.

"You little fucking Devil," she snarled, her voice a stinger injecting venom into the air.

"You cut up my bo —" he began to say in defence, but before he could finish she was on him.

She hauled the covers off and swung the clippings like a whip. The barbed thorns bit into his exposed flesh like tiny knives as she struck again and again, making his skin leak in thin red rivers onto the bed sheets.

"Devil!" she chanted, repeating the word with each strike, her eyes wild and bloodshot. Sam squirmed and scooped himself tight into a ball, an armadillo without the armour.

She only stopped whipping when the clippings lay snapped and broken in her hand, Sam's body a twisted canvas of blood and rose petals. She dropped the bloody clippings to the floor and left, returning a moment later with a box of plasters. Sam tried to weep, but his breath wouldn't catch in his lungs.

"You'll live," she said, throwing the box onto the bed. "Wash it off in the shower. If anyone asks what happened, you fell into the bush."

She left him there, beaten and bleeding. After several minutes his breath returned.

He wept.

After he had cleaned the blood away, he applied plasters to the worst of the wounds. His chest and stomach sported hundreds of superficial nicks and scratches, but his arms and shoulders had taken the brunt of the attack. There were shallow gashes and rips all over them, and a few places where the thorns were still embedded in his skin.

He listened between sobs as his mother grabbed the phone at the bottom of the stairs and called his school, informing them that Sam would be off due to a terrible sickness. She didn't mention that it was *hers*. Blossom had beaten him before, but he had never seen the kind of fury she unleashed that morning. He had glimpsed murder in her eyes. If she had been holding something more solid in her hands, he was sure he would be dead.

His father Griffin had died many years ago, when Sam didn't know what dying really meant. When he was old enough to wonder where his daddy was, Blossom told him his father had died in his car, along with a woman she would only ever refer to as 'The Whore'. He had assumed it was a crash, but later found out, through town gossip, that the car hadn't been moving at all. Someone had stabbed them both multiple times, in a car park on the outskirts of town.

Police never found the killer, although they didn't have to search very hard to find motives. It turned out that Griffin was a reckless gambler, spending most evenings dining at the poker table instead of the dinner table. Police assumed he owed some impatient people who had gotten tired of waiting.

Sam suspected another culprit, however. He always found it odd that his mother refused to acknowledge Griffin, despite the tragic circumstances of his death, and when she did mention him she was more likely to *spit* his name than speak it.

Had she killed his father for his sins? Did she want to kill Sam too? Why? Was it because he was his father's son? Because he reminded her of his betrayal? The real reason, he suspected, was far scarier.

Maybe his mother was just evil.

The next few days, which Sam spent lying in bed covered in plasters, gave him a lot of time to think. Every shift of his muscles, every movement of his body drew a constellation of pain across his skin. Sam wanted to show his mother how it felt to be in so much pain, but he had never been a brave boy and he was certainly not capable of violence. Sam was kind and thoughtful and mild-mannered, virtues shared by many of the heroes in the books he read. He could try a prayer, then. God hadn't listened to Sam before, but maybe he would this time.

Sam knelt at the side of his bed as gingerly as he could, resting his elbows on the mattress. It had been a while since he had done this. He thought for a moment about what to say. He wanted to ask for an abandoned satellite to fall out of the sky onto his mother's head, or for a previously undiscovered volcano to erupt directly underneath her as she pruned her garden, but these were silly requests. Besides, he wasn't even sure he wanted to hurt her. Anger was a passing emotion, after all. As far as Sam knew, nobody existed in a perpetual state of anger, not even the very worst of people. After he had cut her rose bush, he felt regret. But it was too late by then.

His mother would surely forgive him one day for the desecration of her beloved rose bush, and one day in the far flung future Sam would forgive her for beating him bloody with the remnants of said bush. His religious studies teacher, a dour man with a sad smile and a handlebar moustache, told him that good men are forgiving. In this case, Sam thought that forgiveness was still a ways off, but not entirely impossible. Besides, revenge was not a wish New Testament God was known for granting. Instead, he put his palms together, closed his eyes, and simply asked that Blossom got her roses back and then left him alone, which seemed like a perfectly reasonable request considering the circumstances.

That night, every time Sam was jolted by pain, or woke sweating after a vivid nightmare, he said a few more prayers. To God, Allah, Zeus and any other fucking god that would listen.

*Just to be sure.*

The next morning, Sam removed his old plasters, which were caked in sweat and blood, and replaced them with fresh ones. Then he carefully made his way downstairs for breakfast. When he got there, he found he was alone. He listened carefully. There was nothing. Even the television was off.

Was she gone? Was he on his own? Sam thought of the scene in *Home Alone*, when Kevin McAllister wished his family away and woke up the next morning to an empty house. He stepped towards the front door, and as he did it swung open so hard that it struck one of the walls with a loud bang.

"Shit!" Blossom cursed, barging past him over to the sink.

"What's wrong?" he said, startled.

"Get me a towel, quickly!"

Sam went to the drawer under the kitchen window and pulled out a tea towel. He glanced out the front door and saw something that wasn't possible.

*This can't have happened*, he thought. He briefly wondered how long he had been sleeping, but unless he'd been out for months there's no way they could grow so fast. He had cut the heads off with a clear foot of stem below them, which should have put any notion of flowers to rest for at least another year. Probably even two.

But there they were, standing proudly atop the bush like little trophies.

"Give me the towel!" his mother shouted, snapping him out of it. "Damn thing nicked me."

She cradled her forearm under the sink tap. Sam saw that she was bleeding and wanted to say something sarcastic like 'join the club', but he really didn't want a confrontation right now.

"How are they back?" Sam said.

"Go upstairs." She said, through gritted teeth.

"I haven't eaten yet," he pleaded. His stomach let out a timely grumble of agreement. "Can I have some cereal?"

She waved him off dismissively. "Just take the box upstairs." Sam took one more glance at the rose bush and went to his room. He climbed onto his bed and lay down, plucking handfuls of corn flakes from the box and shovelling them into his mouth.

Had she gotten a new bush? No, she wouldn't do that. His granddad planted it for Blossom a few weeks before his sudden death, so she would never replace it.

Sam felt an overwhelming sense of unease deep in his stomach. Not because the flowers had somehow grown back, but because the ones that did weren't the same colour as before.

They were *pitch black*.

The doctor arrived the next day. He was in his late fifties, mostly bald with a salt and pepper goatee. He shook Sam's hand firmly, introducing himself as Dr Reese. The old man glanced at the plasters on Sam's arms and elected to ask no questions about them, which Sam was eternally grateful for.

Dr Reese carried a small brown bag which Sam imagined was filled with a variety of medical paraphernalia. Several bottles of pills were in there too, based on the rattling sound it made when the doctor walked. When Sam opened the door to his mother's room, he stepped back from the entrance and allowed the doctor to go in alone.

"Ms Hargreaves?" Dr. Reese asked softly. Blossom was on the bed, and she turned to look at him. She had large dark bags under her eyes, and she was covered in sweat.

"It itches..." she whispered, running one hand up and down her arm, fingers bent like a leaf rake. There were raised bumps all over her skin, almost like goose pimples, except these were the size of marbles.

"Okay, let's take a look," the doc said, sitting sideways on the edge of the bed. He unclipped his bag and took out a small notebook and pen. "Describe the feeling for me if you can."

"It burns, like a rash, except it's underneath my skin," she said, her voice begging. "I feel like there's an army of ants marching through my veins, and I can't reach them. Please, you need to give me something to get rid of it..."

Sam saw Dr Reese scribble in the notepad. He saw the words 'sub-dermal' and 'persistent'.

"I'll see what I can do," he said, his voice a tenor of practiced sympathy. "What about the bumps on your skin, are they new?"

"They've been getting bigger," Blossom said, focusing on one and scratching it hard. It bobbed around like a tiny balloon, filled with something thick and glutinous. "Bigger and itchier."

"May I see?"

He leaned over and pushed his glasses further up his nose. Blossom held her arm out straight for him. He poked, prodded and probed the biggest bump with his pen. He made no observations out loud, aside from a few soft hums under his breath.

"Looks like a bug bite or a sting of some kind. I'll give you some ointment for the itching, should keep it under control. I'd suggest washing your sheets in case it's bed bugs.

Let me know if it persists or gets worse, but honestly it doesn't look like anything life-threatening."

Dr. Reese said his goodbyes, and left. As he closed the door behind him, Sam hoped the good doctor was correct in his diagnosis.

The ointment lasted about eight hours before it was gone.

It had only stemmed the itching for a little while, but then it returned twice as bad. No matter how much Sam's mother applied, the bumps continued to grow and dry out, and now some of them were enormous. They sat proud on her arm, a mountainous diorama with the skin pulled tight and sore, like bunches of bright red grapes. Some of them stood absurdly tall, and they reminded Sam of the old Looney Toons cartoons, where Wile. E Coyote would be hit in the head with an anvil and a big lump would sprout out with birds and stars flying around it. Something deep inside him wanted to push it in with one finger, if only to see if it popped out again on the other side.

Dr. Reese arrived for a second visit later that day, after Sam had called on his mother's behest, and this time his curiosity was piqued.

Reese finished pulling on his thin blue latex gloves. "Tell me if this hurts," he said, and squeezed one of the largest bumps on Blossom's arm.

It reacted in a way none of them expected.

There was a small puff of powder that flew out into the doctor's face, who coughed and waved his hand at it. Then a viscous yellow-green liquid spilled from the tip, dripping down her arm.

"It hurts, it hurts!" his mother shouted, her other hand grasping at the bedsheets.

"Okay, I'm sorry," Dr Reese said sympathetically. "I'll be quick if you can tough it out for me."

He squinted through his glasses, watching as several cracks appeared near the tip, running down to the base of the growth like the skin of a red banana. Then it split open with a wet pop, and the flaps of broken skin fell against his mother's arm like slices of bloody gammon. She screamed as if she was on fire, and the rest of the lumps followed the first, popping and splitting like tomatoes on a hot frying pan. Each one let out a puff of particles, filling the air.

Sam slapped his hand over his mouth to stifle a scream of his own, and the doctor leapt backwards so fast that he lost his balance and tumbled to the floor.

"Oh my god," he said, his voice shaking. "I've never seen anything like this."

He stood and hurried out of the room, seizing Sam by the arm and dragging him out too. Dr Reese shut the door behind him, stifling the ongoing screams of Blossom.

"What's going on?" Sam asked.

"Has your mother travelled out of the country in the past two months?" Dr Reese gasped. He wiped a handkerchief across his face, cleaning off a concoction of sweat and powder.

"No, we've never left this town."

"Has she been behaving differently or changing her routines at all?"

"No. Always the same."

"What about these?" The doctor said, pulling up one of Sam's sleeves to reveal the plasters.

"I... I was messing around and I fell into mother's rose bush out front. The thorns scratched me up pretty good."

The doctor looked at him sceptically, but after a few moments he dropped his gaze and began gathering his thoughts. He paced back and forth, the only noises coming from his shoes scuffing on the carpet and the muffled screams of his mother behind the bedroom door.

"Son, I need you to keep that room shut and stay out of there until I come back. I don't know what this is, certainly nothing I've ever seen or read about in my forty years, and I must find out before anyone else comes into contact. It might be something exotic, or it could be a hybrid disease. Hell, it could even be a completely *new* phenomenon altogether." He chuckled a little as he thought of something.

*Probably wondering if the new discovery would be named after him*, Sam thought.

Dr. Reese continued, "Either way, it could be contagious, so we can't risk spreading it."

Sam nodded. The wide-eyed panic (or was it excitement?) on Dr Reese's face scared him.

"Do you understand what I'm saying? Don't go in there. Don't touch her. I'm going to my office to call some people who can help. Do nothing until I come back."

"What if you don't come back? What do I do?"

Dr. Reese placed a hand on Sam's shoulder and looked him in the eye. "I'll come back," he said. "I promise."

The first few hours of waiting were the easiest, but after hour six Sam began to worry. The constant whimpering and occasional wailings of his mother were maddening and he wished he could help, but he had not yet broken his promise to the doctor.

After the noises from inside the forbidden room ceased

at around the tenth hour of waiting, Sam began to wonder if the doctor had forgotten about him. Maybe he was still trying to find out what disease Blossom had caught? Or maybe he *had* found out and now he was staying away. Would that be worse?

Either way Sam had to make up his mind. Should he look inside, just in case she was better? Or should he listen to the doctor's advice and stay clear?

It was the not knowing that was driving him crazy. He supposed he had to check on her, if only to make sure she wasn't limbering up on the other side of the door, getting ready to shoulder barge it down and beat him to death. After all, he wished this mysterious disease on her, hadn't he? He sent an angry wish out into the void and someone — or something — had granted it.

He told himself it would only take a second; a simple, casual glance into the maw of Hell, and then he would know for sure.

The short walk to the master bedroom felt like a long and arduous trek, and Sam made it like a death row inmate making his way to the execution chamber. He paused at the bedroom door, taking a moment to gather himself, then grasped the handle. He turned it slightly and winced when there was a stark metallic squeaking from the mechanism. The sound sang like an industrial choir in the still air of the house.

Finally, when the handle was all the way down, he pushed the door ajar.. The stench was immediate and staggering. He gagged and covered his face with his forearm to keep it out, but as soon as his mother came into view around the door his arm fell back down. His jaw followed it.

She was laying still on the bed, the covers pulled up over her stomach. The street light just outside the bedroom window leaked in through the drawn curtains, casting shards of warm orange light over the room. Blossom's arms were completely covered in growths now. Some of them had opened up like the first, while others were bulging great bulbs, waiting for their turn to bloom.

There were other wounds too, where sharp protrusions had ripped through the skin of her arm like shark teeth. Her upper torso was horribly thin, with the growths and thorns spread across her collar and chest, hanging limply against her skin, some as big as golf balls. Sitting atop the form of his mother wasn't her usual skeletal face, however.

Her head was an enormous rugby ball sat atop the hilariously insufficient structure of her neck, as if someone had grabbed her around the midsection and squeezed like you would a toothpaste tube, sending all her contents to the top. The wrinkles she had once sported around her brow and in the corners of her eyes were now gone, pulled taut by the extra surface area. Her greying hair lay in discarded strands on the pillow around her grossly inflated head. Her bald crown was so tightly stretched that he could see the intricate maps of thin blue veins just beneath the surface.

Sam's lungs tightened suddenly, and he realised that he hadn't breathed since he entered. When he did, he immediately regretted it. The aroma was a smorgasbord of different things that should not be combined. Strong fruity smells were followed by the faint notes of decay, and the warm smell of off meat was quelled by a sudden wave of rotting popcorn. It was a Hell all its own, and one meant for the nose.

"Mother?" Sam said, creeping closer to the bed. There was no response. He studied her chest, searching for signs of life. It didn't rise or fall enough for him to see in the twilight of the bedroom, so he leaned in close to listen.

As he turned his cheek to her face, his mother blinked her eyes open. They were bloodshot and lit with madness, and they pierced his own eyes like hot needles. Sam staggered backwards and caught his back hard on the bedside table, knocking the wind from his lungs. Blossom shrieked and sat bolt upright, her face twisted and agonised, then lurched over the side of the bed towards him.

When she emerged from the covers he saw that the rest of her body hadn't escaped the attention of the disease. There were growths protruding from everywhere. Her back and her collarbones were sprouting spikes and bulbs every couple of inches, and he could see bumps in her nightgown where the rest of them hid mercifully from sight.

She dropped to the floor with a soft thud, crawling after Sam. The bony spikes along her forearms scraped the floorboards as she moved, leaving thin scratches along the wood. Sam saw one of the bulbs on her shoulder burst open, spilling a mixture of pus and blood onto the floor.

Sam tried to scramble backwards, but it was too late. She caught hold of his foot. Her grip was vice-like, and he felt a surge of pain as a thorn growing from her palm impaled the flesh above his ankle. Sam tried to catch his breath, but he was panicking now. He needed to break free and get out of the room. Sam threw his arm frantically under the bed, grasping for anything hard and heavy.

His fingers brushed against something smooth and he pulled it out. He could hardly believe his luck! It was a whiskey bottle, with about a quarter of the liquid still inside it. He slammed the base of the bottle down on his mother's hand and felt something crack. She shrieked and yanked her hand away, ripping a wider hole in his ankle.

Despite his bleeding foot. Sam tried to stand, and was horrified to see his mother was trying the same. Her head lolled around like a balloon on a stick, too heavy for her skinny neck to support. She had to use her good hand to hold it up high enough to see him.

She came at him, the growths on her legs jangling like baubles on a morbid Christmas tree. Her thighs and lower legs were emaciated beyond reason, no more than a skin coloured coat of paint directly over her bones. Her bulging lips parted in a rictus grin, revealing stubs of wonky teeth poking from pustulant gums.

Sam swiped at her with the heavy bottle, but she snatched it from his hand with unearthly quickness and threw it. It hit the door behind him, smashing loudly, and the sour odour of strong whiskey filled the air.

Blossom mumbled, her tongue flapping like a fat grey maggot trying to escape from her swollen mouth. The words were illegible, yet Sam recognised the venom in them.

*You did this, you little fucking Devil...*

"I didn't," Sam protested. Tears filling his eyes.

But he had done this, he was sure of it.

His mother reached for his throat, but to do so she had to move her hand from her head. The fluid-filled sac that was once her forehead immediately sagged over her right eye, like left-over gravy sliding from a pan. The sudden loss of vision must have thrown off her perception, and her thorned hand whipped past the soft skin of his neck and slid across his shoulder, tearing as it went.

Sam shouted in pain and tried to shove her away, but she was too strong. She brought her head up to look at him, swiped at him again, and this time she caught him on the side of the head.

He felt a stretching sensation across his forehead, and his vision went red as blood cascaded down his face. He reached up and felt something soft and wet - a flap of skin - coming away from his brow.

His foot skidded on the whiskey covered floor and he lost his footing, falling hard onto broken glass. His shoulder blade lit up with red hot pain as a piece of the broken bottle pierced his flesh near his shoulder blade. He didn't know how big the shard was, or how deep it reached into his back, but he had to fight off the sudden urge to faint. He had never been stabbed before, as is the case with many twelve-year-olds, and it was stranger than he could have ever imagined. It felt as if someone had taken their finger and poked it into his flesh so hard that it pushed the fabric of his shirt inside his body. The pressure and heat was immense, nauseating.

Sam wiped his hand across his face, clearing some of the blood, and he gasped when he spotted his mother bearing down on him. She was coming forward, the bony framework of her skeleton helplessly following her disproportionate head as it fell towards him. She was going to land on top of him.

And then what? Sam didn't want to find out, so he grabbed the first thing within reach, put it between himself and her falling body, and closed his eyes.

There was a wet shucking noise Sam didn't recognise, followed by a cacophony of wheezing gurgles, and then it stopped. He opened his eyes to see his mother had landed on top of him. Her one visible eye was locked onto his, though the fire in them was quickly fading. Sam felt something hot and wet on his chest, which turned out to be blood.

His first thought was that she had eviscerated him, broken him open like a mince pie with her thorns, and he searched frantically with his eyes for his spilled organs.

*His filling.*

He didn't find anything, and realised the blood wasn't his. When she had fallen towards him, he had instinctively snatched the broken whiskey bottle from the floor beside him, and was now gripping the neck so tightly that his fingertips had turned white. On the opposite end, pointed upwards and away from him, was the base of the bottle. The glass was jagged along the lower half, and it was this end that was now embedded into the underside of his mother's chin, opening her throat like a slit in a water bed.

A crimson cascade escaped her body in great gouts of arterial spray. Some of it was pouring and funnelling through the void of the bottle, coming out through the other end in staggered, chugging glugs. The penny-like smell of blood assaulted his nostrils, mingling with the sweetly decay in his mother's last breath.

Sam turned on his side and put the bottle against the floor, before sliding out from beneath her.

The lip and collar of the bottle wedged along a groove between two floorboards and remained upright, balanced precariously. It propped up Blossom's impaled chin, as the rest of her body sagged lifelessly against the floor. It looked almost as though she were performing some kind of hideous yoga technique.

Sam stood, his knees shaking, and drew in several long heaving breaths. He felt as though his lungs were full of fibreglass threads, each gasp forcing his body to shudder like a struck tuning fork. He took a step towards the door and heard a loud hiss that halted him. At first, he didn't know what it was, but when the hiss came again, louder this time, he found its source.

His mother's head was moving, or to be more precise, the *skin* of her head was. Waves pulsated beneath the inflated flesh, rippling down from her crown to her chin.

Sam thought of the way a bowl of water sent out ripples when a droplet landed in it. There were angry red splits appearing from an opening at the very top of her head, running vertically downwards like the segments of an orange.

One line ran perfectly along the centre of her nose and mouth, halving her bulbous face into two equally horrible parts. Another hiss came as the hole at the top peeled open further along the red splits, letting out a puff of particles into the air.

The splitting skin curled, opening the top of her head like the petals of a lily, Sam's favourite flower. He watched as it hissed again, revealing the magnolia gleam of bone beneath.

Her head was peeling open.

Thick strands of sticky red mucus stretched between the flaps as they pulled away from her skull. As Sam watched, helpless, her head folded open fully with an almighty rip. The thick petals of head-flesh settled against her dead shoulders with a soft slap, glistening wetly in the sodium vapour of the streetlamps. Sat in the centre was her skull, perched on the ruined remnants of her head like a priceless treasure on a red velvet pillow.

There was something beautiful about the final form her body took as it expired, but all Sam wanted to do was run away. He felt something salty drip over his top lip, mingling with the coppery blood, and he realised he was crying. Not just crying, but bawling. His emotions exploded out of him like a burst dam, an overwhelming tide that poured out unbidden.

He bolted for the door, needing to be out of this room, needing to be anywhere else other than here.

As he pulled it open he saw Blossom's skull tumble from

its perch, clattering to the ground. It sounded like someone dropping a bundle of wet sticks. Her skull tumbled end over end, before coming to rest against his foot.

"I'm sorry...." Sam blurted, turning away from his mother's empty, accusatory eye sockets.

Sam stumbled out of the front door into the night air. It was dark, but he did not know the exact time. It felt like he had been inside that room for hours.

Even though he was far from the bedroom where his mother's absurd corpse lay, he could still smell the sweet, musky aroma of her decay, clinging to him. He tried to stop the bleeding from his various wounds, but there were too many to count and his head was a churning vat of nausea. The gash on his brow had slowed, but the blood around his eyes had turned dark and sticky. Every blink became a concerted effort.

There was a deep, haunting throb somewhere near his shoulder blade, and when he lifted his arm he could feel the muscles in his back bunching up against some kind of barrier. He guessed it was the shard of broken glass he had fallen on.

His ankle gave way each time he attempted to put weight on it, giving him a lurching limp when he opened the front door and plodded out onto the garden path. Sam glanced at his mother's rose bush and saw that the flowers had bloomed, a crimson core burning within the black petals like a hot coal in a log burner. He staggered towards the bush and snapped off every single flower, dropping them onto the ground. He stepped on them, crushing the delicate petals under his heel.

"This isn't what I wanted," he said quietly, though he wasn't sure to whom.

Another noise caught his attention, a thrumming hum from somewhere beyond the garden. He followed it, and saw a car parked against the kerb. Its engine idled gently, but the lights were off.

Through the dim auburn light of the street lamp he could see a figure in the driver's seat; the vague silhouette of a man, with his head tilted back on the headrest as if he were taking a quick nap. Sam hobbled closer and tapped the glass.

The man gave no response.

"Help..." Sam whimpered, his voice hoarse. "Help me."

Nothing. He tapped harder, begging. "Please, help me..."

The man didn't flinch. *Was he okay in there?* Sam cupped his hands over the glass and leaned his face into them, hoping to see who was inside.

He saw, and he screamed. The figure flinched into life at the sound and Sam jerked away, falling to the ground. His backside thudded hard against the pavement. He wheezed frantically, his breath evading him.

The door of the car swung open and Dr Reese flopped out. His head was swollen and bleeding just like Sam's mother's had been. Hard black spikes and bulbs of flesh covered his face and hands.

The thing that had been Dr Reese mumbled incoherently, but the words clogged in his mouth, trapped behind the wads of bloody yellow mucus that oozed from his scabbed lips. He manacled his hand over Sam's leg, the thorns on his palms digging into his shin like the barbed teeth of a leech.

Sam didn't scream. He had no breath left to do so. He had just enough time to wonder whether Dr Reese had even left at all earlier that day. Sam supposed it didn't matter. Either way, the doctor had kept his promise. He *had* come back, and now he was climbing atop Sam with madness and desperation in his eyes, his body ripping and bursting and blooming like a flower of flesh and blood.

## BIG HAIRY THIGHS

THERE ARE THINGS ABOUT CAMPING FOR WHICH I DON'T CARE,
    but they said "Get back to nature, you'll find yourself
there".


I tried for an hour to put up a tent,
    ripped one of the sides and the poles were all bent.
    I struggled and stressed and let out a scream,
    Then with a monstrous yell,
    threw it into a stream.


I found a hollow log and tried to refrain,
    from crying in despair when it started to rain.
    It was dark and cold on that damp forest floor,
    tormented by noises and, one time, a roar.


My blood ran cold and a chill climbed my spine,
    when I heard something massive walking nearby.

It sniffed and it searched for the source of my odour,
until it lifted the log and my hiding was over


The beast was enormous and hirsute and strong,
I thought it was myth but I was clearly wrong.
Some call it Sasquatch or Yowie or Yeti,
but the best way to describe it is 'hairy and sweaty'.


Bigfoot's Big Feet matched his Big Hungry Eyes,
and his Big Gnashing Teeth matched his Big Hairy Thighs.
He broke me in two and carried me off,
as I choked and sputtered and pleaded and coughed


We arrived at a clearing after an hour or more,
where he dropped me like garbage to the moss-covered floor.
It was here I discovered an unwelcome surprise,
who'd have guessed Bigfoot had several Bigwives?

# THE DESPICABLE THING

Owain Cadogan was, at his deepest essence, a decent man. Over the years, however, he had matured into something terribly cynical and miserly.

Sat upon the cobblestones of Benllyger, a rural Welsh town in the heart of the valleys, Owain spent his mornings and afternoons as a street beggar, dozing in the hazy sunlight.

The locals were familiar with Old Owain, as they were familiar with the mining accident that tragically crippled him years before. Many of the townsfolk were miners themselves, and they sympathised enough with his plight to hand him food and coins whenever they could spare them. To them, Owain was nothing more than a tragic example of fate's unkindness; someone who had been dealt a cruel hand and collapsed under its pressure, and they tolerated him out of pity.

The local children, however, had a great fondness for Old Owain. Mostly because he slipped them a few coins every so often, so they could buy candied sweets from the local confectioner. Owain was sure to throw in a few lewd jokes to guarantee the rowdier youths a laugh, and he would even let the more curious of them poke at his crippled legs with sticks.

When evening fell, Old Owain would pack up his belongings and hook his wheeled cart to a malnourished pony, who pulled him dutifully to the local tavern. There, his day's worth of pity would pay for a few hours of drunken merriment, until it was time to go home. His routine had remained unchanged for years, and Owain had grown comfortable with it.

One night, however, Owain's journey went very differently.

Very differently indeed.

He was no more than twenty minutes from home, full of ale and craving his bed, when he felt an intense sense of unease in the pit of his stomach. The pony evidently felt the same way, because it whinnied and whickered at every rustle of grass and whistle of wind that passed through the hedgerows.

Something, it seemed, was following him on the opposite side.

If the pursuer was attempting stealth, it was not succeeding. He heard the thing breathing heavily on the other side of the hedgerow; a thick rattling, as if someone dropped a handful of stones on the skin of a drum. Clumsy, oddly timed footfalls broke twigs and sploshed in the mud, and Owain assumed it must be a curious cow or a territorial bull.

He barely had time to finish this thought when the thing burst through the hedge, ripping and snapping the thick green branches like hay-stalks. The unusually large and misshapen silhouette was difficult to see in the dim light of the oil lamp affixed to his cart, but still Owain was stunned by its size and sure it was not of bovine lineage. It easily exceeded seven feet tall, if not more.

Old Owain's pony snorted in panic and neighed loudly. The noise seemed only to enrage the mysterious beast, which pounced on top of his pony with a furious roar, sending the cart tumbling over. Owain fell into the cold dirt like a spilled sack of potatoes, his belongings scattering across the ground.

The dark figure roared again and tore at the pony, ripping and throwing great chunks of flesh aside. It didn't take long for his late companion's dismayed cries to subside, and the monstrous creature turned to Owain. He knew immediately who — or rather what — his assailant was.

"My God…" Owain muttered, aghast and afraid.

It stepped further forward into the pale light, revealing its grotesque visage in full. It was a Ffachen Giant, a fabled and fearsome creature of the hills. The sprawling woods and valleys had been Owain's playground as a child, and he would regularly disappear amongst the trees to investigate tales of cunning sprites and beasts of myth. The Ffachen Giant was a particularly terrible creature, whose myths were filled with blood and violence. Owain had enjoyed them with an unusual glee, which he now regretted.

These brutish monstrosities were said to be born with only half of a true body; they owned a single leg, on which they hopped gracelessly. In the centre of their barrel chests they sported a single muscular arm, ending in a clawed hand that could tear a man's flesh like sheep's wool.

The head, misshapen and bulbous and matted with stringy puffs of thick red hair, was home to a thin mouth, a large nose, and one lonely, lidless eye staring wildly from its deep socket. The monstrous deformities lent the giant a legendary rage, and a feral jealousy of symmetrical things.

The Ffachen fixed Owain with its baleful gaze, and let out an ear-splitting roar. Owain's heart shuddered from the sound, and the sinister thing's malodorous breath washed over him in a foetid wave. He started to retreat, heaving himself backwards with his arms, but the towering creature set back on its single thigh and leapt forward. It landed with a heavy crash in front of him.

In a cacophonous, bellowing voice, it spoke. "Where do you think you're going, human?"

Owain gave no response aside from howling in terror, his whole body shaking like a shitting dog. There was a twisted smile spreading across the Giant's crooked mouth.

"I... I... don't want to die," Owain stammered.

"Oh, you won't die!" The Giant said, almost reassuringly. "At least not promptly. No... first I will tear off one arm and one leg."

Its rough tongue licked out at blistered lips, relishing the idea.

"Then I'll pluck out an eye with one of my fingernails."

"No..." Owain whimpered.

The creature's own bloodshot eye flicked toward the cart. It picked up the huge wheeled contraption with no effort, inspecting it. The heavy wooden object looked minuscule in its massive grip.

"What is this?" It asked.

"It is for m-my legs..." Owain replied.

"A cripple?" The Ffachen laughed, a hideous basso sound that rumbled the bones inside Owain's body. "Even better! Maybe I'll let you keep both of your legs, or maybe I'll crush them into a single pulp with my fist. I wager you wouldn't even feel them break."

"Wait, please," Owain begged, holding up a hand. "If it's a wager you want, let us make one!"

The hideous creature stopped and thought for a moment. Ffachen Giants were said to have a propensity for gambling and bargaining, and Owain reckoned on only one chance of escape.

"I may consider a wager," the giant boomed. "But the contest will be of my choosing. If you are victorious, you will be spared."

"Very well, but you must give your word I will be let go, and you shall not accost me again so long as I live."

The giant's eye flicked hither and fro as he considered. Eventually he laughed again. "You have my word. My terms... are that you must beat me in a simple race."

"A race?" Owain snorted at the audacity. "I may be giddy with fear but I am no imbecile. I am crippled!"

"And I am unbalanced and unsteady. Neither of us are creatures of haste or poise, yet the victory is still surely mine. We race to that tree." The creature pointed it's gore coated hand, and Owain looked into the darkness to see the canopy of a great oak tree against the light of the moon.

It was close.

"You are a despicable thing, monster. I have no choice but to agree to your terms."

The crippled man and the deformed thing lined themselves up for their contest, and the beast broke a wooden branch in its enormous fist to signal the start.

The Ffachen Giant, huge and half-witted, watched in confusion as Owain got to his feet and ran, rather more quickly and nimbly than his age should have allowed, down the old dirt track.

The great lumbering beast attempted to give chase, but stumbled on its precarious leg. It fell to the ground with a bewildered grunt.

Old Owain, out of breath and gasping, placed his hands on the gnarled trunk of the wise old oak. He had won.

He turned and walked back to his cart.

"How...? Your legs!" The Giant said, glaring angrily with his watery eye.

Owain Cadogan, who had never been crippled, smiled. He leaned down and picked up his half-spilled sack of coins.

"You are not the *only* despicable thing that lives in these hills."

## DODIE

DODIE DOESN'T KNOW WHAT HIS CAPTORS ARE,
    or what they want.


They speak an odd language
    that Dodie doesn't understand.


Sometimes, they tie Dodie up by the neck
    and drag him through the streets.


Other times, they make Dodie perform simple tricks
    for their amusement.


The tall and ugly things seem pleased by his obedience
    and they offer him rewards.

.  .  .

So Dodie sits, Dodie begs, Dodie rolls over and plays dead,
all the while plotting his revenge.

# THE ELGIN INCIDENT

DID YOU EVER HAVE ONE OF THOSE LITTLE RUBBER BOUNCY balls when you were a kid? I did. I had this kick-ass red one that bounced so fast and high that it was probably too dangerous for a child under the age of ten to play with. I loved that fuckin' thing.

My mother took great pleasure throwing it in the bin after three broken windows and two black eyes for my brother, who often insisted on being in its flight path. I was devastated. I remember thinking, all those years ago, that my abusive relationship with rubber was over.

As a police detective, I saw some heavy shit before my retirement. I've investigated sick-fuck serial killers, been stabbed twice, shot at more times than I can count. Hell, I've even killed people in my career. Bad guys, of course, although that doesn't make it any easier to pull the trigger.

But you wanna know the shit that keeps me up every single night? The one bug I can't wipe from my windshield? The one *man* whose name still makes me nauseous when I hear it?

Stuart Elgin.

That motherfucker is my Freddy Krueger.

Dispatch called me up that night to coordinate and control the site of 'an accident' with multiple fatalities. That's all they said. Easy peasy, right? Looking back on it now I should've figured there was an unknown element, otherwise they would've just sent the meat wagon to collect the bodies and left me to enjoy my god-damn Frappuccino.

The address was a Research and Development Facility on the outskirts of town, one of those secretive grey buildings where science-types piss about with things they shouldn't. The victim was a professor by the name of Stuart Elgin, head of R&D for Crescent Laboratories. These guys were big players in the science world, leading the field on all sorts of fancy boffin shit. They'd even appeared in the national news a few years before, for inventing a special environmentally friendly plastic that became the industry standard for soda bottles.

That's some impressive shit, right?

Well, Elgin's newest project was an attempt to increase the elasticity of rubber - to make it stretchier and bouncier and... I don't know, rubberier? Based on what we know now I guess you could call it 'ill-fated', but honestly that doesn't seem fair considering he technically succeeded. *Technically.*

Christ.

I still see that lab every time I close my eyes, like the whole fucking mess is tattooed on the back of my eyelids. It was total chaos. Every surface in the lab had at one point been pure white, but the constant spray of blood had speckled them almost completely red. When I walked in I practically tripped over the corpse of a woman who, it turned out, had been the first to discover the Professor after his death.

Her skull was cracked open, with the soft pale grey of

her brain showing through the cavity like the surprise toy in a human Kinder Egg. All of her limbs had been snapped, some so violently that the bones poked through the skin like sharp teeth from bloody gums.

Professor Elgin's body was close by, inside a small cordoned-off area. The walls and floor looked as if they had been painted with a thick brown substance, which I quickly concluded was some sort of rubber. Partly because I'm a very intuitive detective with great instincts, and partly because Elgin's body hadn't yet stopped bouncing on it.

His corpse, mangled and utterly wrecked by this point, was being repeatedly smashed into the ceiling again and again, his body sticking for a split second before peeling away and falling back down. Each time he bounced, the impact was accompanied by a loud wet crunch, like someone stepping on a bowl of cheesy nachos. It sounds cliché to say this but I can still hear that fucking sound in my head when it's too quiet.

Elgin, in all his wisdom, had pulled what we started to call 'a Flubber', after that Robin Williams movie. Not very sensitive, I know, but there's only so much blood you can see outside of the human body before it starts to affect your sense of humour - call it a 'coping mechanism', or whatever. Elgin hadn't just increased the elasticity of the rubber, he had invented the absolute most rubbery rubber in the whole fuckin' universe.

He was over the moon with his breakthrough of course, until he tripped over a beaker or a Bunsen burner or some other science-class bullshit. I bet he survived those first few bounces, at least long enough to regret everything he had ever done. But that ceiling was solid concrete, and it made pretty short work of his body.

First thing I did was bring in CSI to examine the scene

and take samples, but I must have accidentally hired Beavis and Butthead because these two idiots wouldn't listen to a fucking word anyone told them. You told them to sit, they'd stand. You told them to walk, they'd run. You tell them to tread carefully around the super-elastic death rubber, and they stand on it immediately.

In the blink of an eye Professor Elgin's solo performance had turned into a macabre ballroom of tumbling, broken bodies. There were four fatalities now - two under my watch - and I still had no clue what to do. The Professor's body was starting to look like a well-fucked blow-up doll that desperately needed a top-up, and the two CSI boys were well on their way to being closed caskets too.

So that's when I had the bright idea to bring in the bomb squad. I know there wasn't technically 'a bomb', but I wasn't about to let another human being near that compound, and I know that the bomb squad had those little robots with the remote controls. I figured they could send the damn thing in to get a sample of the rubber, so we could find out what exactly we're dealing with, right?

Well apparently — and I wasn't aware of this — those robots aren't as sturdy as they *look*, and they're pretty fucking expensive too. When that little metal bastard touched the rubber, flew across the room, and smashed into a million pieces against the wall, I felt the assholes of every member of the police budget committee clench at once.

So we were back to the drawing board again. We sat around for hours, trying to come up with a new plan, and that's when the suits finally rolled in. It was only a matter of time, and to be honest I was glad to see them. I could tell that the constant thumping and crunching was disturbing some of my officers. The smells too. It's odd that people don't really talk about those, because they never leave you either. That sickly-sweet odour of human death, mixed with the chemical tang of a laboratory - it lingers in your nostrils, clings there like a parasite.

The Feds cordoned the whole site off and shut it down like it was Area 51. They made every one of us sign a Non-Disclosure Agreement too, although it didn't take long for someone to sell their story to Buzzfeed. After that went live, this nightmare became a sort of internet urban legend. According to one of the article's sources, Professor Elgin had figured out a way of 'activating' the molecules of the rubber compound with an electrical charge, agitating them into super-elasticity until the charge was 'turned off' again.

Sounds like mumbo-jumbo, but it makes sense to me. Especially when you consider all those wild stories coming out of the Middle-East.

There's all this talk of flamethrower type weapons that pump out liquid goop, launching insurgents into the air like they were on a fucking trampoline. Other guys I've spoken to say they've seen rubberised armour that literally reflects bullets back at the shooter. My personal favourites are the mysterious black ops soldiers who can leap over small buildings in a single bound like Clark fucking Kent. The grunts call those guys 'Spring-heeled Jacks', apparently.

I can't really say for sure if those reports are true. The only thing I know for sure is that, whatever the truth is, it'll come out soon enough. That's one of the good things about having a complete narcissist running the free world, he can't help bragging about his new toys. One of these days he'll blurt out something about Elgin's compound on social media and that'll prove us 'crazies' right.

If you ask me, we shouldn't be fucking around with things like that. *Science isn't always an exact science,* that's what Stuart Elgin taught me.

## THE ETERNAL THICKET

THERE IS A SECRET FOREST
   on the outskirts of town,
   where the desperate are called
   so to never be found.


It is hidden from most
   and graces no map,
   it exists within a sort of
   'temporal gap'.


It is a gloomy old place
   from Autumn through Spring,
   where the insects are still
   and the birds never sing.


When a person arrives

with intentions to end,
a voice from the forest
whispers to them.


It asks them to "stand very still
and wish very hard,
for the Gods in the leaves
will turn skin into bark."


"A tree will be borne
from the soul left behind
until body and vine
are forever entwined"


It is a simple offer,
and many have picked it.
The newest recruits
to the Eternal Thicket.


There are rows upon rows
as far as can see,
an army of people
who, now, are a tree.


It is easy to tell
if you know where to look,
when this curious process

has been undertook.


If you feel quite so brave
    as to climb up the trunk
    you'll see shapes in the bark
    where their faces are sunk.


Arms become branches,
    and fingers grow thin,
    if you snap them in half
    you'll find bones are within.


I suspect you have doubts
    about a story so strange,
    but there is one little detail
    you'll never explain:


When the process begins,
    and their bodies are taken,
    It is a very quick thing
    and they rarely are naked.


Whatever they wore,
    when the forest took hold,
    still adorns their new form,
    and a story is told.

·　·　·

Some branches sport gold,
  or some count the hours,
  and most of the trunks
  are still wearing trousers.

# BURY US

I ALWAYS THOUGHT I'D BE A GREAT SURVIVOR.

After the boat sank, we handled the situation pretty well, all things considered. Sure, Carl had a few moments of despair that he tried (and failed) to hide, and I cried only when he was asleep. Despite that, we mainly kept our shit together.

Our first *real* moment of panic came when we found that damn portable toilet.

It was just sitting there in the forest, a giant blue rectangle plonked in the undergrowth like an absurd monument to the human turd. Initially, we were overjoyed. Toilets meant civilization, civilization meant people, and people meant *rescue*.

I still remember the way my stomach sank when Carl pulled open the door. The miasma of odours was so vile that it should have killed us instantly. The toilet *was* occupied, but its occupant wasn't. Not anymore, anyway. The dead man was slumped in the seat, his head rocked forward as if bowing, limp arms dangling lifelessly between his legs. A pair of shorts lay bunched around his ankles. He had clearly died on the job.

What made matters worse was that the sun had beaten down on the toilet for God knows how long, turning it into a big plastic oven. It was so hot that the dead man's skin had melted, sloughing off his bones like thick custard from an upturned bowl.

It was Carl who first noticed the weeping sores on the man's neck. I pointed out the boils on his legs — soft lumps protruding from the skin as if it were a balloon inflated beyond its capacity.

I think that was when we realised our luck had soured.

Carl suggested we travel a little deeper into the forest, and I agreed. We followed the sound of flies until we stumbled into a large clearing. I vomited, and Carl began to cry. On the far side of the open clearing, in complete opposition to the lush greenery around us, was a small soundstage. On it, a DJ booth was left unmanned. Power was still being fed through from a generator somewhere, and the multi-coloured lights hanging on the rigging above the stage still whirred around, soundless and aimless, like frantic eyeballs searching for something.

There were bodies everywhere.

In front of the stage, presumably once a makeshift dance floor, were the motionless forms of shirtless young men and bikini-clad girls. The once-vivid neon glow-sticks accessorising their bodies had long since dimmed, replaced by bright red sores and open, festering wounds. Some were missing limbs; others, eyes - taken by birds and other scavengers.

Carl and I agreed that this small, isolated island had likely been used to host an illegal rave for rich kids — somewhere there were no neighbours to disturb, no police, and no rules to adhere to. An adventure, a party and a nightmare, all-in-one.

It looked like the disease had spread quickly and spared no-one, killing them fast. So fast in fact, that most had seemingly died in the midst of doing something else. There was a bartender lying dead behind his bar, still clutching a glass in one hand. Behind the stage a man and a woman lay on top of one another, both of them dead, both of them naked. They had been fucking when it took them. Whatever this affliction was, it was rapid and devastating.

By the time we realised the contagious nature of the disease, it was far too late for Carl. He was already showing symptoms. He denied it at first, of course — stubborn as a mule, that one — but I could tell. Back at the beach camp, I saw him cough up a clot of thick, dark blood which he tried to cover with a handful of sand.

Within a few hours, Carl's skin turned a shade of agitated red, and the inflamed sores started to emerge. Soon, he could barely see out of his swollen eyes, and he had taken to sobbing all through the night.

Thankfully, I hadn't shown any signs of the mysterious disease, so I insisted on keeping myself isolated from him. I created a second shelter on the opposite side of the beach, and I tried to keep as quiet as possible. I realised that if I didn't make any noise, Carl wouldn't be able to find and infect me. He would still cry out in pain all night and day, and I often heard him stumbling sightlessly in the dark. He never discovered my shelter.

I actually started to resent him. It wasn't really his fault, but he made life on this island more difficult than it needed to be. He would leave long trails of blood and pus in erratic patterns up and down the beach, turning my daily survival into a sort of macabre version of hopscotch.

After a few nights I lost track of him, and I assumed he had wandered into the sea to die. My suspicions were confirmed when I saw his body lolling in the shallow waves one evening. It was surrounded by small crabs, scavenging at his bloated corpse, their red claws plucking away ragged pieces of grey meat and feeding the wet morsels into their chittering mouths. Carl was so grossly inflated that I expected to come out of my shelter one morning to find he had exploded. Instead, his body just disappeared, mercifully dragged away either by the waves or the wildlife.

I thrived for so long without any signs of illness that I began to think I was immune. I began to wonder if there were other survivors on the island, from the rave. I decided to go back and explore the clearing where we found the kid's bodies. I discovered another area just beyond the first, where rows of tents were left abandoned. There were several crates of tinned food, along with a few cases of energy drinks and alcohol. Enough to survive a few weeks, maybe long enough for help to arrive.

That remained the plan for another week, until I realised the truth of my situation. It was so plainly obvious that I'm surprised I didn't realise it sooner.

I cleared away the S.O.S sign Carl and I had built out of rocks. It seemed pointless to keep it there. When it was gone, I bent over and coughed, then kicked some sand over the dark clot of blood.

I haven't seen another boat or plane since I arrived here, and I don't think I ever will. This whole place is forsaken. Do they know what's on this island? Is that why nobody came for those kids? Maybe they can't risk the disease leaving the island.

I'm writing all of this down now to occupy my mind. I'm getting worse with each passing hour. I've started to lose my motor functions. Exhaustion has robbed me of my will. I've given up waving off the crabs, who refuse to wait for my death. They've taken two of my toes already, and they gather in greater numbers every day.

If you're still healthy, get off this island. It's too late for me, but *you* can survive. Tell someone we died here.

Bring us home.

Bury us.

# ACKNOWLEDGMENTS

Thanks first and foremost to you for buying this book and reading it for so long that you ended up on this page. It's frankly amazing to me that this book exists at all, let alone that anyone would read it.

Thanks to my wife, for always having my back no matter what. We've been through a lot of shit, but we are slowly approaching the day you can tell your friends that you married a failed author!

Thanks to Vlad Beaverhausen, for reading 'Flower of Flesh and Blood' and advising on its more sensitive content.

Last but by no means least, very special thanks are due to David Sodergren — my editor on this book — who waded through my prose, picking out the bones and bits of hair until it looked good enough to eat. Thanks mate, you're the man. Check out his books *The Forgotten Island* and *Night Shoot* if you get a chance!

# AUTHOR'S NOTES

SO YOU MADE IT TO THE END! IT'S GREAT TO SEE YOU HERE, you look amazing. Did you style your hair differently?

Anyway, I'm sure you're here to find out What The Fuck Was I Thinking When I Wrote That, so why dont we cut to the chase?

*The Great Travelling Graveyard*

This story was inspired - in part - by a *Magic: The Gathering* card called 'Corpseweft'. It's a spell depicting Liliana (a necromancer) summoning a rampaging blanket of zombies at her opponents. I thought that the word was so interesting and vividly descriptive on its own that I wanted to write a story about it. Although, I obviously took a very different direction in my telling! Is this the nerdiest story origin of all time?

·  ·  ·

*Curse Word*

I've always been fascinated by the way people react to swearing. As the saying goes; *sticks and stones may break my bones, but words will never hurt me.* But what if they could?

*Truffles*

This will sound strange, but I have no idea where this idea came from. I wanted to enter a competition in a Facebook group called 'Fiction Writing', so I started writing with no preparation, stream of consciousness style, while I lay in the bath. This is the story that came out. You're right, it is worrying.

*The Ballad of Slippery Reese*

I had a funny idea about writing a story surrounding an outlaw in the old west who couldn't be hanged, no matter how many times the Sheriff tries. I wrote two drafts of the story and both were terrible, so I instead turned it into this bizarre little poem. I think it works better.

*The Clump*

There is nothing I hate more in this world, nothing that

repulses me on such a primal level, than pulling my wife's hair out of the plug hole in the shower. It's ridiculous because it's probably the cleanest hair in the world, right? It gets washed twice every day!

*Kiddo*

Kiddo was written in about an hour, for a 500-word story challenge in the aforementioned Fiction Writing group. I just had a log burner fitted in my house, and decided to write a story based around one while the fire crackled and popped in the background.

*Flower of Flesh and Blood*

I wrote this story in 2013, for the reddit page r/nosleep. It was originally in first person perspective, and it was arguably the worst short story anyone had ever written. I pulled it from the bin, gave it a dust-off and a shiny new perspective, and this is what it came out as! I'm proud of this story, even though it exposes my undying love for body horror!

*The Despicable Thing*

Being Welsh is great in many ways. We eat loads of cheese on toast, and we have a lot less negative space on our road signs than English people. The main downside is that we have the crappest mythological creature of all time; the Ffachen Giant. I wanted to write about one of these odd beasts in the style of an old folk tale or a fable, because I grew up reading them! I have a soft spot for this story, despite its silliness.

## The Elgin Incident

What if someone invented *Flubber*, but it went horribly wrong? Enter Stuart Elgin. This was my first ever story acceptance, and I still struggle to understand why. It's *Flubber*, if *Flubber* was an episode of *The X-Files*.

## The Eternal Thicket

A fantasy story I scrapped a long time ago had a scene in which the characters visited 'The Eternal Thicket', a copse of trees made up entirely of humans who had given up on life and gave themselves to nature. A scene in the movie *Annihilation* reminded me of this, and I adapted it into a poem instead. I couldn't help adding a bit of tongue-in-cheek humour though, as is my curse.

## ABOUT OWEN MORGAN

OWEN IS A WRITER FROM SOUTH WALES IN THE UK. HE specialises in flash fiction and short stories. His first Flash Fiction / poetry collection *The Great Travelling Graveyard and other brief tales* was published in October 2019.

He is also the co-owner of The Abominable Book Club Ltd, the UK's only horror fiction subscription box.

You can follow him on twitter @ON_morgan or on insta-gram @on_morgan_, where he is liable to talk about horror movies, professional wrestling, and dumb ideas for stories.

Printed in Poland
by Amazon Fulfillment
Poland Sp. z o.o., Wrocław

50516028R00060